Book Four

Angus&Robertson
An imprint of HarperCollins*Publishers,* Australia

First published in Australia in 1998
by HarperCollins*Publishers* Pty Limited
ACN 009 913 517
A member of the HarperCollins*Publishers* (Australia) Pty Limited Group
http://www.harpercollins.com.au

Based on the television series 'Li'l Elvis Jones and the Truckstoppers' © Australian
Children's Television Foundation, Australian Film Finance Corporation, Kalidor Pty Ltd
trading as Viskatoons, France Animation, Ravensburger Film & TV Gmbh and France 2.

Published in association with the Australian Children's Television Foundation.

The illustrations in this book were drawn by Peter Viska with help from Edo Fuijkschot,
James Dunlevie and Wen Xiaoquan.

HarperCollins*Publishers*
25 Ryde Road, Pymble, Sydney, NSW 2073, Australia
31 View Road, Glenfield, Auckland 10, New Zealand
77-85 Fulham Palace Road, London W6 8JB, United Kingdom
Hazelton Lanes, 55 Avenue Road, Suite 2900, Toronto, Ontario M5R 3L2
and 1995 Markham Road, Scarborough, Ontario M1B 5M8, Canada
10 East 53rd Street, New York NY 10032, USA

National Library of Australia Cataloguing-in-Publication data:

Marker, Steve.
Monkey sea, monkey do : It's a dog's life.
ISBN 0 207 19656 7.
I. Title. II. Li'l Elvis Jones and the Truckstoppers (Television program).
III. Title: It's a dog's life. (Series : Li'l Elvis Jones and the Truckstoppers ; 4).
A823.3

Printed in Australia by Griffin Press Pty Ltd, Adelaide on 80 gsm Econoprint

10 9 8 7 6 5 4 3 2 1   98 99 00 01

Book Four

Li'L ELViS JONES
and the Truckstoppers

Monkey Sea, Monkey Do
and
It's a Dog's Life

Retold by Steve Marker
Illustrated by Peter Viska

From the original screenplays by John Armstrong and Robert Greenberg, and Pepe Trevor and John Armstrong

Angus&Robertson
An imprint of HarperCollins*Publishers*

Theme Song

Lyrics: Ralph Strasser Music: Bruce Rowland

Len: Here's the story, Sonny Jim . . .
And I swear every word is true . . .

To a Flaming Star, on a desert night
In a Cadillac of golden light
On the floor by a truckstop door He left a prize
A rock 'n' roll surprise for Len and Grace
A little baby boy in a guitar case
The new mum and dad could hardly
    believe their eyes

Grace: And as the Caddie vanished into the night
I was sure we'd been touched by The King!

Li'l Elvis: So they called me Li'l Elvis
And Mum reckons I'm the son of The King!
Li'l Elvis!
I was born with a gift to sing!

So with Janet and Lionel, we made a band
Spreadin' Didgibilli music across the land
And I swear every word is true . . .
The Truckstoppers!
And Li'l Elvis Jones

Len: Thank you very much!

Monkey Sea, Monkey Do

MONKEY SEA, MONKEY DO

The puppy in the window of the Dove sisters' general store really believed that now, at last, his loneliness might end. He had remained in the window for what seemed like centuries. The Dove sisters were kind to him, but nothing could hide the fact from the puppy that he had neither owner nor name.

And now three children were staring in at him. One was a girl with mauve-tinted glasses, another a boy with a red bandanna across his forehead, and the third an odd looking child with thick orange hair but kindly eyes. It was this third child who, in the puppy's opinion, was the person most likely to rescue him. He widened his eyes and tried to look as appealing as he could.

'He's so cute, isn't he?' sighed Li'l Elvis Jones to his friends Janet and Lionel.

Lionel shook his head. 'Li'l Elvis, I don't trust anything that doesn't have an on-off switch.'

The puppy widened its eyes even further as Li'l Elvis turned to Lionel.

'You always say stuff like that, Lionel, but I know you're really a pet kind of kid.'

'Sure I am,' Lionel replied sarcastically.

Unnoticed by the children, the puppy resorted to desperate measures. It sat up and pressed its front paws together to beg.

'Well, I'm going to get a pet, no matter what!' proclaimed Li'l Elvis.

'Oh yeah?' put in Janet. 'And what are Len and Grace going to say about it?'

The puppy did a somersault. The children paid no attention.

'Janet, don't worry about them,' answered Li'l Elvis. 'See this finger, they're so wrapped around it, they'll do whatever I say.' He held up his little finger and set off for the roadhouse.

'This I've got to see,' said Janet, as she set off after him.

The puppy tried its last and most desperate manoeuvre. It did a triple backflip — something only a few puppies are capable of doing — and banged its head against the window. It struggled slowly and uncertainly to its feet, eyes finding it difficult to focus.

Lionel caught sight of the puppy and was nearly overcome by pet-craving himself. 'Oooh . . . cute,' he cooed.

But he realised just in time what was happening and snapped out of it. He glanced all around to make sure that no one had noticed, and set off after his friends.

The puppy resigned himself to more lonely namelessness.

★ ★ ★

Just outside Little Memphis, stood Desolation Plain, perhaps the best place in the world for anyone wanting to go really fast in a motor car. Except for the occasional lizard, it was usually empty. But now it seemed positively crowded.

A woman peered into a camera, microphone in hand and began to talk quickly in a voice so strident that on a quiet day it would have been heard for kilometres. 'Eileen Innyaface, Junk News, here at Desolation Plain, where daredevil Herb

"Brittlebones" Petrankovic is preparing to break the world land speed record in his nuclear-powered vehicle, "The Nukebird"!'

Seated in what looked more like a rocket than a car, was a man with a thin moustache and a very daredevilish glint in his blue eyes. He smiled at the camera.

'So, Herb, tell our audience what this big red thing is for?'

Eileen reached down, and grabbed a red lever on the dashboard.

'Don't touch that! It's the —' Herb reached for her hand, but was too late. Herb shot out of the cockpit in a cloud of smoke. 'AAAAAAaaaaaaaarrrrr . . .'

'Wow, an ejection lever.' Eileen patted down her hair. 'Anyway, this event is proudly sponsored by Moore Industries. Remember, Moore is better, more Moore is best.'

Eileen pointed to a huge advertising banner showing the grinning face of WC Moore, the billionaire with flair. At that moment, Herb struck the banner, and since it broke his fall, he landed on the ground without suffering any serious injuries.

'And now,' began Eileen, once again speaking into the camera, 'here are some highlights of Herb's previous record attempts . . .'

'First there was the Moonshine Bird ...' commentated Eileen.

TV screens all around the country showed Herb falling heavily to the ground. This time he must have broken several of his brittle bones.

Next came a racing car with what appeared to be a huge oven stuck to the back.

'Then there was the Microwave Bird,' came Eileen's voice-over.

A bell rang, sounding like an oven-timer, and the car again blew up. Herb once more crashed to the ground.

The next car looked sleek and far more modern.

'Then of course, the Berkonium Bird,' continued Eileen.

This one hardly moved at all before exploding. Again Herb was thrown high and fell down heavily.

One of the millions of TV sets showing these pictures stood in a corner of the roadhouse living room in Little Memphis. Behind the counter, Len, L'il Elvis's dad, watched the screen with a dreamy expression.

'Ah,' he sighed, 'they just don't make cars like that anymore.'

Li'l Elvis and Janet shattered this thoughtful atmosphere by shooting into the room on their scootboards, only just avoiding a collision with the counter. Li'l Elvis straight away began his campaign to get a pet.

'Dad, can I have a puppy? Can I? Can I?'

'I think . . .' said Len indecisively, 'that you should go ask your mother.'

Janet laughed mockingly and held up her little finger to remind L'il Elvis of what he had said about having his parents wrapped around his finger.

'Nyah, nyah, nyah,' she taunted.

Li'l Elvis glared at her and stomped off to find his mother. Janet remained behind, caught by a picture on the television. This was black and white, and so belonged to ancient history. It showed Herb with someone who looked very like — no, *extremely* like — Len.

It *was* Len.

Herb, whom Janet recognised immediately as the famous high-speed driver, had an arm casually around Len's shoulders. On Len's overalls was a picture of Herb, criss-crossed with spanners.

Janet's eyes widened. 'Uncle Len? Is that *you* with *Herb Petrankovic*?'

'Yep,' Len answered dismissively. 'Ancient history, Janet.' But behind his dark glasses his eyes gleamed with the memory of that exciting ancient history.

A vacuuming sound came from behind the door to Li'l Elvis's room. This was a bad omen because his mother was never in a good mood while tidying his room. Nevertheless, he pushed open the door.

'Mum,' he protested, 'I told you I'd clean up my room.' A banana skin lay right in the centre of the floor. Grace narrowly avoided stepping on it.

'That was two years ago, Li'l Elvis.' Grace continued to shovel the cleaner back and forth. 'There are some forms of life that I'd prefer not to have in this house.'

Once again, she just missed the banana skin. Despite his mother's mood, Li'l Elvis decided to come right out with it . . .

'Speaking of life forms . . . can I have a puppy?'

Grace swung around, again stepping very close to the banana skin.

'No,' she said. 'You've got no sense of responsibility at all. You can't even keep your room clean. You certainly can't look after a puppy.'

She was about to leave, but Li'l Elvis moved in front of her, nearly making her step onto the banana skin.

'Then what about a kitten?' he begged. 'A guinea pig? A highly disciplined earwig?'

'No, no, no. Now out of my way. I have to get a mop.' She left the room.

'Rats!' Li'l Elvis sat on his bed in a huff. He stared ahead, defiant rather than discouraged, saw the banana skin, and angrily hurled it out of the room.

From the corridor came a scream and a crash as one of Grace's feet finally found the piece of pure fruity slipperiness. Li'l Elvis raised a hand to his mouth, ran out, and found his mother on the floor of the living room, drenched in dirty water and with the mop on her head like a wig. Len and Janet had gone, but the TV was still on. Grace glared at her son, who couldn't help continuing his campaign.

'I take it it's a bad time to ask for a gold fish?'

Grace growled.

Li'l Elvis was backing away when Scotty, a man wearing bright tartan clothes with a thick Scottish accent, loomed up on the TV screen.

'Mooms and Dads, does your wee sprog keep pestering you for a pet? Well, if you dinna think your kiddie is up to the responsibility of a wee beastie, think again!'

Scotty produced an aquarium full of strange creatures, like miniature monkeys, swimming underwater. Some were wearing crowns, others were playing guitars.

'Sea monkeys!' shouted Scotty. *'The fantastic aquatic sensation sweeping the nation! And they're maintenance free!'*

Li'l Elvis gave Grace his most hopeful, pleading look. Grace merely scowled.

'And for just twenty dollars,' continued Scotty, *'a whoole colony of these happy wee chappies is yours!'*

'Artist's impression only,' said a voice on the TV, very quickly.

'Soo,' came Scotty again. *'Don't be a sporrin kicker. Buy your wee sprog some sea monkeys today.'*

Grace stood up slowly, shaking droplets of mop-water from her hair. Li'l Elvis jumped onto a bar stool and brought his face as close as he could to his mother's. Like the forgotten and nameless puppy in the window of the general store, he widened his eyes.

'Mum? Are you a sporrin kicker?'

'All right.' Grace finally gave in. 'You can have some of those monkey things, but you'll have to find the twenty dollars yourself.'

Li'l Elvis pushed his hands into his pockets. Perhaps, perhaps . . .

But all he came up with was a twenty cent piece.

Then Janet and Len rushed in.

'Grace! Look what I found in the shed!' shouted Len.

Len was wearing the overalls that had just been on television, showing the picture of Herb with crossed spanners underneath. Janet was wearing a cap with same emblem.

'We're the Petrankovic Pit Crew,' she announced proudly.

'Come on!' urged Len. 'We don't want to miss it!'

Janet and Len grabbed Li'l Elvis and Grace and took them outside.

The television was left alone in its corner of the room, broadcasting a picture of a graceful white spacecraft in orbit around the earth. Who was filming this scene? Another spacecraft?

'*And coming up*,' came the voice of Eileen Inyaface, '*a defence spokesman denies claims that Space Lab is a spy satellite . . .*'

A small grandstand had been erected on Desolation Plain beside a souvenir stall. But there was no crowd on the seats; everyone was gathered around the Nukebird, soon to make an attempt on the world land-speed record. Duncan, WC Moore's pathetic chauffeur, stood a touch too close to the jet-like exhaust, and found his face covered by soot.

Hector and Victor, two of Little Memphis's shopkeepers, stood at the souvenir stall, holding up T-shirts with Herb's face on them.

'Getta your "I SAW HERB BREAK THE RECORD" T-shirts here!' called out Hector.

He tried to put one on, but found that it would not get past his head. He waved his arms as though trapped in the T-shirt, but no one paid him any attention.

WC Moore had climbed to a podium in front of the grandstand.

'Ladies and gentlemen, Moore Industries takes great pleasure in introducing a very close personal friend of mine — Frank Petrankovic!'

Herb jumped onto the podium, wearing white overalls and with his hair and thin moustache neatly brushed.

'It's *Herb*, by the way,' he murmured to WC.

WC shrugged indifferently.

'Hello Little Memphis!' Herb called to the crowd.

The crowd cheered. Herb leant forward, looking closely at one of the many faces before him.

'Len!' he shouted. 'Len Jones you ol' pit stop hound dog! Is that you? And . . . Gracie?'

Herb jumped down and led his old friends onto the podium, where he hugged them before the eyes of the crowd.

'It's been a long time, Herb!' said Len.

'Lenny,' Herb patted his friend's back, 'you're still the best darn mechanic I ever had — and I'm still wearing that watch you gave me!'

He rolled up his sleeve to reveal a watch about

the size of a coffee mug, made of whirring, pumping, spluttering machinery. He held it up to the crowd.

'Len made it out of the carburettor from my very first wreck! I've worn it on every record attempt — it brings me luck.'

'But haven't you exploded every single time?' Grace couldn't help asking.

There was silence, until Len coughed. The watch's mechanical noises suddenly stopped. Herb started it again by pulling at a cord. Black smoke gushed from the watch's exhaust.

Li'l Elvis and his friends were paying no attention to any of this. Li'l Elvis was explaining avidly to Janet about the sea monkeys.

'That's right. For ten bucks each we can own a colony of sea monkeys!'

'Monkey fish?' Janet screwed up her face. 'Sounds horrible.'

'Drowning monkeys,' said Lionel cynically. 'Yeah, great pets, El.'

At the podium, Herb did a running jump straight into the seat of the Nukebird. Eileen was waiting for him with her microphone.

'Herb? Nervous?' she asked.

'No, Eileen,' Herb explained patiently. 'Everything is planned down to the last detail. For example it's vital that I start at exactly three o'clock — not one second earlier or later.'

'Why is that? Weather conditions? Angle of the sun?'

'No, the crew astrologer reckons Jupiter is in my second bungalow.'

And indeed over there, near the grandstand, at a table all by herself, filing her fingernails over her star charts, was Madam Rita, the crew astrologer. Beneath her fingernail dust lay a map of the future which only she was capable of reading.

Herb's watch had begun to beep.

'And that's my lucky watch saying it's time to go!' announced the brave driver as he revved the engine.

The Nukebird zoomed to the starting line.

Grace, on the podium, glanced at her own watch.

'Len, why is he starting now? It's only half-past two.'

Len shook his head ruefully. 'That watch never did keep good time.'

Madam Rita, too, having heard the Nukebird's motor, was checking her watch. When she saw the time, she gave a mystified frown. There had been nothing about this in the charts.

'Two-thirty?' she wondered.

She stared down at her map of the future and in it she saw disasters and triumphs, happiness and

misery, each and every thread in the tapestry of human experience . . . including a disaster for Herb if he didn't start his attempt at exactly three o'clock.

'Uh oh! . . . Herb! Herb!' She jumped up and ran towards the starting line. 'Come back! You've gotta come back!'

But the Nukebird's nuclear engine was roaring far too loudly for Herb to hear what Madame Rita was saying. He waved back to her and wound the power-dial on the dashboard to eleven.

★　★　★

Way, way up above Desolation Plain, in the airless darkness of space, the Space Lab was orbiting the Earth. Doors opened and a giant mechanical arm unfolded, holding a spy camera of about the same size and shape as those used to take holiday photographs. A flashbulb went off. 'Whoops. Left the lens cap on again,' a smooth computerised voice said apologetically.

Another arm unfolded and tried to remove the lens cap. But it seemed to be stuck. The arm exerted greater force and finally the lens cap did come off, but so did the arm.

It was a huge robotic arm and as it fell towards Earth it waved goodbye to its twin.

Down, down, plummeted the arm, getting hotter

and hotter as it tore through the Earth's atmosphere.

It seemed to be heading for Australia, for just about the middle of Australia, in fact for . . .

★ ★ ★

The Nukebird was screaming across Desolation Plain, but Eileen, the television reporter, was making nearly as much noise as she shouted into her microphone.

'And this is incredible, the Nukebird's just nano-seconds away from the world record speed!'

Everyone in the grandstand was sitting right forward, watching anxiously.

'He's gonna do it . . .' muttered Len. 'This time he's really gonna do it!'

The Nukebird's speedometer was heading resolutely for a zone marked in red. Anything in this zone would be the fastest anyone had ever travelled on land. Herb pushed his foot hard against the accelerator.

But what was that, high in the sky? Edged with flames and glowing red-hot, it appeared to be . . . a gigantic mechanical arm.

The people in the grandstand stared up, then down at the Nukebird. The speedometer needle was nearly, nearly in the red zone.

'Yes! Yes!' shrieked Eileen. 'He's done it! Herb Petrankovic has broken the world record!'

Herb looked up.

He barely had time to wonder what he was seeing before the Nukebird and the space-arm collided, igniting the fuel rods in the car's nuclear engine and making an orange blast, a flash of light, and finally a mushroom cloud over the desert.

Everyone was too stunned, at first, to know what was going on.

'I didn't agree to pay for any fireworks,' growled WC Moore on the podium.

A breeze blew away the mushroom cloud and Desolation Plain returned to being flat and empty. There was no sign of Herb or of his car.

At the souvenir stall, Hector and Victor were the first to recover. They hastily stamped their T-shirts with a mushroom cloud and Hector's cry broke the silence: 'Getta your "I SAW HERB GET NUKED" T-shirts here! Getta your "I SAW HERB GET NUKED" T-shirts here . . . '

★   ★   ★

Len was on the living room couch, hands over his face sobbing. It was the next day, but he was still wearing his original 'Herb's Pit Crew' overalls.

'Herb,' he was lamenting. 'My old mate . . . Kaboom . . .'

Grace and Elvis were doing their best to console him.

'Len,' Grace said soothingly, 'you mustn't blame yourself. Just because it was your watch that sent Herb to his death . . .'

Len sat up straight, startled. 'Geez . . . I hadn't thought of that.' He began to cry even more mournfully.

Li'l Elvis stood up. 'Maybe the TV will take our minds off things.'

He turned it on, only to see Eileen sobbing into her microphone.

'A memorial service for the late Herb Petrankovic is to be held tomorrow. And may I extend my personal condolences during this tragic time.'

She suddenly cheered up.

'And after the break, a wacky way to recycle old underpants!'

Li'l Elvis switched it off.

'Li'l Elvis?' Len managed to ask, sniffling. 'Can you go and buy a wreath for the memorial service tomorrow? Here's twenty dollars.'

He held out a twenty dollar note.

'Twenty d-d-dollars?' Li'l Elvis stammered.

The sea monkeys had become more to him than just pets in a tank. He had begun to think of them as friends rather than pets. He imagined himself underwater with them, singing while they played guitars:

'We're the sea monkeys!
The ultimate consummate pet!
Sea monkeys!
We're like chimpanzees but we're wet!'

Li'l Elvis went straight to the general store and, ignoring the puppy in the window, asked Dotty about wreaths.

'This,' the old woman explained patiently, 'is the wreath you can buy for twenty dollars.'

The boy pushed the large flower and leaf arrangement aside.

'What can I get for twenty cents?' he asked eagerly.

★ ★ ★

Cast hastily in solid bronze, the town's monument to Herb was about three metres tall and showed a mushroom cloud with Herb's head emerging from the top. Li'l Elvis stood before it, holding the wreath that he had bought for twenty cents. It consisted of a single wilted carnation, the stem twisted into a circle. The card attached said, 'In Sympathy. From Len, Grace, Janet and Li'l Elvis'.

He picked up the card from the hugest wreath at the base of the monument. 'In Deeply Tortured

Grief and Endless Sorrow. From WC Moore,' it said.

'Yeah right,' muttered Li'l Elvis sceptically.

He switched the cards and ran off.

Behind the massive monument WC was playing marbles with Lionel and Spike. He loved the game because he owned a powerful Berkonium marble that allowed him to always win.

Duncan approached his master. 'They're waiting for you to give the eulogy, boss.'

'In a moment, Duncan.' WC flicked his Berkonium marble, which curved beautifully, hitting every marble in the circle, and sending them into his pocket. Obediently, his Berkonium marble flew back to his finger. 'Boys,' grinned WC, 'when it comes to flicking glass, I'm the man with class.'

Lionel and Spike screwed their eyes tightly shut, more enraged with themselves than with WC. Why on earth did they agree to play with this obnoxious man? It was the challenge, they supposed. One day, one day, they would beat him.

WC went around to the other side of the monument and peered down at the wreaths. He saw the tiny one with the card attached.

'*That's* the wreath I payed for?' he bellowed.

And without giving Duncan the chance to defend himself, he zapped his loyal employee with his 'communication' watch, a watch that he wore for just this purpose.

'Yeowww!' cried Duncan.

The podium was just down the road, a small crowd had gathered around it. Opposite, the nameless puppy watched from his window as WC jumped up and began his speech.

'Good people of Little Memphis. We're here today to honour Kev Petrankovic. A great friend, a great Australian, a great explosion . . .'

★ ★ ★

As the Jones family returned to their roadhouse after the memorial service, Len shook his head angrily.

'Did you see that miserable wreath WC Moore bought?'

Li'l Elvis looked guiltily away, in time to see a delivery van roar up and hurl out a cardboard box. He bent over to read the label. '*Caution: Live sea monkeys inside,*' he read out loud. 'Fantastic!'

'Sea monkeys?' Grace wondered. 'Li'l Elvis, where did you get the money to buy . . .'

Before Grace could finish her question, Li'l Elvis sprinted to his bedroom. He tore open the cardboard and peered inside. Way, way, down the bottom were two tiny packets. The label on one said 'Sea monkey food' and on the other 'Mongolian swamp algae'. But this last one had been crossed out and the following words stamped over the top:

'SEA MONKEY EGGS. DIRECTION: PULL TAB OF REDLY HUE. EGGS ARE DROP IN CAREFREE WATER, THEN YOU WAIT. SOON VERY EXCITEMENT AND JOY TO EXPERIENCE.'

'Yeah!' shouted Li'l Elvis. Finally, finally, he had his sea monkeys. 'Okay, here goes.'

He tore open the packet and poured dozens of tiny dried-up eggs into his fish tank. They shuddered as they hit the water, then expanded and stretched out, before exploding in a shower of bubbles. When these had cleared, tiny creatures were wriggling in the water, looking more like worms than monkeys. Li'l Elvis found a magnifying glass and peered at them. Some looked a little like tiny octopi, others like shrimps, but that was about it. When they saw Li'l Elvis's huge eye staring at them, they huddled to the far corner of the tank.

Li'l Elvis threw his magnifying glass to the floor in disgust.

'They're not monkeys at all,' he exclaimed. 'They don't have crowns, or guitars, or even *faces*!'

He fell onto his bed, flicked his legs and sent his shoes (which came off easily, because of their

elastic laces) flying to the ceiling. Then he threw off his socks. One landed in the fish tank, the other on his face.

He still couldn't believe what a rip-off the so-called 'sea monkeys' were.

'I stole twenty bucks for those . . . *worms*? Arrgh!'

Li'l Elvis's dirty sock sank to the gravel in the tank. The sea monkeys stared hungrily at the packet of sea monkey food on the bedroom floor. They tried to swim there, but only collided with the glass.

The next day was hot, even for Little Memphis. Lizards hid from the sun in the cracks between rocks, and the few plants in the desert shrivelled up, hoping that if they pretended to be dead they would escape further torture from the sun.

But the town's school teacher, Lillian Dexter, Lionel's mother, cared nothing about the heat. She took the whole year five class out to Desolation Plain and announced: 'The theme for today is "Getting to Know Your Desert"! So I want you all to go off and find something wonderful for show and tell.'

She had come well prepared for the harsh conditions. She opened her umbrella and a whole garden setting unfolded, complete with banana lounge, side-table and even a cold drink with ice cubes and a straw. She put on sunglasses and sat down.

'Something that expresses the spirit of the landscape,' she elaborated. 'And the person who finds the most exciting exhibit wins a special prize.'

Janet rushed one way, Lionel the other. Li'l Elvis stood still, then went in a different direction. As vulture-like birds circled overhead, he jogged through the desert until he saw his two friends, already at the spot he had decided would be the best for finding interesting exhibits.

The earth was scorched and even hotter than elsewhere.

Li'l Elvis stared at the ground. 'This is where the Nukebird exploded. There's bound to be some pieces of it lying around. We'll win show and tell for sure!'

'Yeah!' called out Lionel and Janet, who had already gone out to search.

Li'l Elvis spotted something glowing bright-green beneath a rock. It was a glowing spanner. He shoved it into his backpack where it stuck out, still glowing.

Lionel appeared, looking sensible. 'Personally, I don't think it's worth risking radiation sickness or genetic mutation just to win show and tell.'

'That's why I'm a lead singer and you're just a didge player. No one else will have anything like this. We'll win for sure,' boasted Li'l Elvis.

On the blackboard of Lillian's classroom was a long division problem that no one had bothered to complete, but on her table was a whole pile of Nukebird souvenirs. Everyone in the class had had the same idea as Li'l Elvis. There was half of Herb's helmet, Herb's glove moulded to the gear stick, and Herb's steering wheel . . .

While the children took their seats, Lillian frowned at the class.

'When I asked for show and tell items,' she scolded, 'I didn't mean charred post-nuclear remains. So, if there's anything else from the crash site, get rid of it now!'

Silently, children deposited further souvenirs — a hub cap, a speedometer with the needle just into the red area, and so on — onto the table. At the back of the class, Li'l Elvis shoved his glowing spanner deeper into his backpack.

'Now,' Lillian asked hopefully, 'is there anything which *isn't* from the Nukebird?'

Spike had been waiting for this moment. Grinning wildly, he rushed to the front of the glass and shoved a two-headed snake into his teacher's face. The heads hissed and bit each other.

Lillian backed away. 'How revolting!'

'I found this, Miss.' Spike advanced closer, snake in hand.

'Fine. You win, Spike.' Lillian, reached behind her. With a swift movement she brought an elephant stamp hard onto Spike's forehead.

'There!' she cried. 'The red elephant stamp of outstanding merit!'

Stunned, Spike nevertheless smiled with gratification, and kissed the doubled-headed snake.

Li'l Elvis wasn't impressed. 'It should have been me,' he muttered bitterly.

After school he went straight home and, still feeling resentful at not having won show and tell, grabbed a tin of cola from the refrigerator and went to his bedroom. He stood over the fish tank, slurping from the can. Everything, lately, had been disappointing.

'Rotten Spike,' he muttered. 'No way he should have won . . .'

The sea monkeys were still wriggling up near the packet of food. Li'l Elvis's sock lay on the gravel, a dreadful greeny-brown slime just beginning to ooze out of it. Sometimes, Li'l Elvis lost count of how many days he wore the same pair of socks.

'Rotten sea monkey worm thingies,' he sulked. 'Rotten twenty dollars for nothing. Rotten sporrin kickin' Scotty . . .'

He dropped the empty can of cola into the tank and fell backwards onto the bed, forgetting that he still had his pack on.

'Ooooowww!' he cried, when the nuclear spanner stuck into his back. He tugged it out and hurled it across the room.

It splashed into the fish tank, joining the sock, the cola can, and the starving sea-thingies.

Li'l Elvis had dinner and then fell asleep. As night swept across the desert, and cooled Desolation Plain, the sounds of washing-up came from the roadhouse kitchen where Li'l Elvis lived.

People were turning on their lights, but Li'l Elvis's window was already glowing.

But not with the normal light of an electric bulb. No, it was glowing *green*. Li'l Elvis lay asleep on his bed.

Suddenly he sat up, woken by the brightness of the light. He shielded his eyes, trying to work out where it was coming from.

Over there. He walked over to the fish tank and stared into it.

The light flashed out, filling the room with a glow so bright that it was impossible to see anything else. Then the room darkened, but Li'l Elvis was no longer standing beside the tank. And his bed, too, was empty as the stars twinkled over the desert.

★　★　★

Morning sunlight lay across the wall of Li'l Elvis's bedroom as Grace appeared in the doorway.

'Li'l Elvis?' she called out. 'I think we should talk about . . . Li'l Elvis?' She saw that the bed was empty and looked about the bedroom, but without seeing Li'l Elvis.

She didn't see Li'l Elvis, but not because he wasn't there.

It was because he was the size of a dwarf mouse and was lying unconscious at the bottom of the fish tank. His mother's voice woke him up. Grace looked huge, magnified by the water and glass.

'Mum? Mum!' he shouted, bubbles coming from his mouth as he spoke.

He ran towards her and collided with the glass wall. 'Oof! What's happening? Where am I?'

He was underwater, yet he had no difficulty breathing. Also, he saw as clearly as if he were in the air or wearing goggles. He heard a strange bubbling growling sound and turned to see a group of sea monkeys behind him.

They looked exactly as they had in Scotty's TV ad, except that their faces were angry. They were the same size as Li'l Elvis and were carrying tridents, which they raised to point at the boy. One, wearing a crown, swam forward.

'Ah!' he exclaimed in a deep voice. 'The human man-child with flaming head! You are now our pet! Guards!'

Before Li'l Elvis could move, he found that he had a dog-collar around his neck, joined to a lead. The king of the sea monkeys dragged him away, swimming, over to where the dirty sock sat in the corner, still oozing concentrated grime.

The king pointed to it. 'Recognise this?' he demanded.

'It's just . . . a dirty sock.' Li'l Elvis tugged at the collar.

'To you, maybe!' The king flourished his trident. 'But to us, it is the Deadly Fungus Mountain, oozing the most evil of poisons.'

He pointed to a group of sea monkeys who were coughing and choking, lying in the shadow of the sock. One tried to move away, but was too weak to do so.

'Onward!' called out the king.

The collar tugged against Li'l Elvis's neck as the king led him to the half-empty cola can.

'And this!' The king pointed with his trident. 'The Cavern of Obsession! The black liquid inside drives my people wild with craving! All they want to do is drink it all day!'

And sure enough, around the other side, near the opening to the can, lay a pile of unconscious sea monkeys with vague smiles on their lips. As Li'l Elvis watched, a sea monkey staggered out with a faraway yet not unhappy look, and collapsed onto the pile.

'Onward!' cried the king again.

He led Li'l Elvis to the green-glowing nuclear spanner, leaning against the glass in the far corner.

'And here,' the king's voice became deep with menace, 'here is the most horrible of the curses that you have inflicted upon us! The Leaning Tower of Suffering!'

'The nuclear spanner! Oh no!' gasped Li'l Elvis.

On the orders of the king, a sea monkey swam into view. As it loomed before Li'l Elvis, it grew another head. Another monkey appeared, forming a third eye above its normal two. The next had two tails, which allowed it to swim twice as fast as any of the others.

'What have I done?' lamented Li'l Elvis.

The king jerked the lead, forcing Li'l Elvis to kneel.

'Silence, man-child with flaming head! I find you

guilty of crimes against the Sea Monkey Kingdom! You are hereby sentenced to *death*!'

'Death? Isn't that a bit extreme?' whispered Li'l Elvis.

'We regard it as appropriate under the circumstances,' replied the king. He grabbed a trident, raised it, and prepared to execute both the sentence and the boy.

'Wait!' cried Li'l Elvis. 'Maybe I can help?' He was thinking faster than he had ever done in his life. 'Maybe I can fix up some of the bad things I've done.'

Thoughtfully, the king lowered his trident. 'Hmm . . . all right. I will give you twenty-four hours! But should you fail — the death sentence!'

'Of course, your Sea Monkiness.' Li'l Elvis gulped, but plans were already forming in his terrified brain.

As Li'l Elvis and the sea monkeys set to work, the tank water became choppy and bubbles swirled about inside. After only a moment's hesitation, Li'l Elvis led them to the sock. He pulled at a thread and the wool began to unravel. He tied this to a sea monkey trident, which he hurled like a javelin at his desk lamp outside the tank. It wrapped around it, before splashing back into the water. He tied the free end around the glowing spanner and the sea monkeys helped him pull the strand. The rod rose slowly out of the tank.

'That's it!' called out Li'l Elvis. 'Heave, monkeys, heave!'

As the rod rose out of the water, the monkeys chanted:

'We're the sea monkeys brave and true,
Flaming Head shows us just what to do,
He's been bad and that's no lie,
Gotta make amends or he's gonna die!'

No one saw that the wool was fraying badly. With the spanner hanging over the edge of the tank, the rope snapped. Li'l Elvis and the sea monkeys fell over backwards and the spanner crashed through the glass wall.

Water gushed out from the jagged hole. The sea monkeys screamed. Without water they would all die.

'Oh no!' cried Li'l Elvis.

Water and sea monkeys spilled out through the hole. Li'l Elvis grabbed a jagged edge and saw the king being swept towards him.

'Your Monkiness! Give me your hand!'

Li'l Elvis caught the sea monkey's hand, but the torrent was too strong. With a frightened look in his once proud eyes, the king was swept to the floor. Li'l Elvis, too, was swept away.

'AAAaaaaarrr . . .' cried the king and the boy.

It was still morning and a heap of bedclothes lay on the floor beside Li'l Elvis's bed. The bedclothes rolled over and a head emerged.

It was Li'l Elvis. 'Oh boy, what a nightmare . . .' he groaned.

The fish tank was intact. Li'l Elvis remembered last night's glowing green light. What *had* happened? He felt that it had all been real in some way and not merely a dream. He caught sight of the glowing nuclear spanner, the sock and the seeping tin of cola still in the tank. Had all these combined last night to push him into a world just as real, yet far more dangerous than his own?

He sung quietly to himself: 'Gotta make amends or I'm gonna die . . .'

He jumped up, grabbed the packet of sea monkey food, sprinkled some in the water, and fished out the sock, can and finally the nuclear spanner. How was he supposed to get rid of this piece of nuclear waste? Wasn't it supposed to stay poisonous for a million years?

He dropped the sock and can into his waste-paper bin and ran down the hall, heading for the back door.

In the kitchen, Len was frying eggs, Grace was setting the table.

'Li'l Elvis,' she began, as her son appeared, 'it's time we talked about . . .'

Li'l Elvis halted. He didn't have much time, what with nuclear waste to get rid of. He spoke quickly. 'The twenty dollars? I stole it and used it to buy sea monkeys but I was sentenced to death by the sea monkey king and boy did I learn a thing or two about responsibility. Sorry, Mum and Dad. I'll pay it back.'

'Err, fine,' mumbled Len, not sure what all that was about.

★　★　★

Still carrying the nuclear spanner, Li'l Elvis whizzed deep into Desolation Plain on his scootboard until he came to a sign. '*Deserted Mine Shaft*,' he read out. 'Perfect.'

Beside the sign was a hole that seemed to go down forever. Li'l Elvis hurled the rod into the blackness and turned to go.

'Ow — that hurt!' came a shout from behind him.

Li'l Elvis stopped and went back. 'Who's that?'

'Who's that?' came the voice, like an echo.

But Li'l Elvis thought he recognised the accent. 'Mr Petrankovic?'

'Yes! Help!'

Li'l Elvis leant right over the mine shaft and looked down.

Herb was only about five metres away, hanging by his lucky watch which was caught on a fragile looking tree root. He was wearing half a helmet and one glove. His anti-gravity suit was badly singed.

'Li'l Elvis! G'day, g'day!'

The tree root shuddered and nearly gave way as Herb called out.

Li'l Elvis reached down as far as he could. 'Whoah . . . give me your hand, Mr Petrankovic!'

'Just call me Herb, all right?' Herb's hand stretched up to Li'l Elvis's, but they couldn't quite meet.

Then Li'l Elvis had an idea. He whipped out the elastic laces from his shoes, tied them together and knotted one end to the sign, the other to his ankle. This, surely, would give him the extra millimetre that he needed to reach Herb.

He leant over the shaft, further and further . . . until he had hold of Herb's hand. He had just started to wonder whether he had the strength to pull Herb up, when he felt himself slipping over the edge.

Herb fell with him.

They careered down, stretching the elastic shoelaces tighter, tighter . . . Then, right at the bottom, inches from the rocky ground, they came to a full stop. The shoelaces gathered their strength, about to whisk them up again.

'Lucky I found you,' mentioned Li'l Elvis. 'Or the ghost of Ol' Man Izard who haunts these caves might have got you.'

'There's no ghosts down here, Li'l Elvis,' Herb just had time to answer, before the upward swing of the shoelaces launched both of them upwards at a speed that was fast even for the famous Herb Petrankovic.

'Whooooaaaa!' cried the boy and the man together.

But the shoelaces' velocity declined as they went up, and deposited them safely on the ground above. Even so, they rolled over and over, and had to wait until a cloud of red dust had settled before being able to see each other.

'Son,' Herb began, 'you did a very fine thing. So maybe there's something I can do for you, eh?'

Li'l Elvis smiled. 'Um, now that you mention it. There's this little competition we have at school . . .'

★   ★   ★

In the Little Memphis classroom, Lillian was writing something on the blackboard, her back to the class, and Spike was dancing around in front of the other children, pointing with both hands to the elephant stamp on his forehead.

'Nyah-nyah-nyah-nyah!' Spike leered.

Li'l Elvis threw open the door.

'Late again, Li'l Elvis,' Lillian scolded. 'Not another invasion by savage homework-eating aliens?'

'No, Mrs Dexter. I've been out getting something special for show and tell — Herb!'

And Herb himself stepped into the classroom, smiling in his daredevilish way.

'Herb Petrankovic!' Lillian cried. 'But you can't be . . . I mean, you were . . .'

'You're a corpse!' Spike accused. 'We saw you get fried!'

Herb gave the boy a patient look. 'Ah, now that's where you're wrong. When I saw that outer space hoosamajigger coming for me, I pulled the big red handle, and ejected just in time!'

'Aw, you're making this up!' Spike wasn't going to give up so easily. 'Big fat liar . . .'

Lillian swung around to the boy. 'That's enough, Spike! I hereby strip you of your merit prize . . .' And with that, she wet her handkerchief and wiped off the elephant stamp.

No longer a child of merit, Spike went slowly back to his seat.

'And I award it,' continued Lillian, 'to Li'l Elvis Jones for his Herb Petrankovic show and tell exhibit!'

She stamped the red elephant onto Li'l Elvis's forehead, and the boy grinned.

Everyone looking at him, so pleased, seemed to remind him of something. A puzzled looked came into his eyes and for a second or two he wondered . . .

'I wonder,' he whispered to himself, 'if that's the way it happened on the night I was found.'

In his imagination he saw Herb roaring up to the roadhouse, late one night. The racing car slowed down and a baby in a padded guitar case was ejected through a compartment in the roof, landing at the feet of Len and Grace, outside the roadhouse.

He shook his head. Would he ever find out the truth about who his real parents were and how he had been delivered to Len and Grace?

That night, Eileen Inyaface again appeared on millions of TV screens, including the one in the roadhouse living room.

'*And so,*' said Eileen in one of her most earnest voices, '*a nation salutes the late Herb Petrankovic! And we'll be back tomorrow night to see if we can milk any more out of this tragedy.*'

A picture of Herb filled the screen, causing Len to rush over and tearfully wrap his arms around the TV.

'Herb, if only I'd never made that stupid carburettor watch, maybe you'd still be here . . .'

A voice with an accent that Len recognised straight away came from behind him.

'But that watch saved my life, Lenny!'

Len spun around. There in the doorway stood Herb Petrankovic, well and truly alive, with Li'l Elvis beside him.

'Herb! You're alive!'

As Len and Herb embraced, the high-speed driver said: 'You've got a great boy there, Len. You should be proud.'

Li'l Elvis's grin was one of the widest he had ever given.

★ ★ ★

That night Li'l Elvis and his band the Truckstoppers, Janet and Lionel, had a jam session in Li'l Elvis's room. First, Li'l Elvis poured some sea monkey food into the extremely clean fish tank.

Janet laughed. 'Li'l Elvis, you've been feeding those worms for ages! They're never going to get any bigger.'

Li'l Elvis shrugged, searching for the right words. 'Look, they're just . . . special, guys. I can't explain it or you'll think I'm nuts.'

'So what else is new?' answered Lionel and Janet.

And then the children began to play their instruments, concentrating far too hard to notice what was happening in the fishtank.

A group of sea monkeys had come out from behind the plastic rock.

Some had guitars, one was wearing a crown, and they were dancing in time to the music. When they had got the hang of the song, they joined in — singing and playing their guitars. Though not quite loud enough for Li'l Elvis Jones and the Truckstoppers to hear them.

It's a Dog's Life

IT'S A DOG'S LIFE

No dog in the whole world could look more vicious than Anzac when he wanted to. He lived with Ol' Man Viska and his job was to protect the junkyard from thieves and vandals. He was famous throughout Little Memphis for his savage temper.

One typically fine desert day Anzac advanced on Li'l Elvis Jones, snarling as ferociously as he could. But instead of running away, the boy remained calm. He was holding a whip made of old rope. He cracked it fearlessly.

'Back you vicious lion,' he commanded. 'Back I say!'

Anzac advanced. 'Graarrrararararar!'

Behind Li'l Elvis were his friends, Lionel and Janet, who were also the members of his band the Truckstoppers. They were sitting on the wreckage of a washing machine. Instead of being concerned for their friend or worried about what would happen to themselves once Anzac had finished eating Li'l Elvis, they looked to be dying of boredom.

'Hey, Li'l Elvis,' Lionel called out, 'this lion tamer thing is getting old fast, you know?'

'Yeah, me and Lionel are bored,' Janet added. 'What about you Anzac?'

Anzac immediately stopped snarling and nodded. He was bored too.

Li'l Elvis shrugged. 'Okay, let's play cute little puppies.'

Anzac's eyes lit up. He loved this particular game. He flipped over and Li'l Elvis began to tickle his tummy.

'Cute little puppy, coochy coochy doggy,' said Li'l Elvis in a high-pitched voice.

'Hehehehehe!' laughed Anzac.

Lionel and Janet, their boredom suddenly gone, jumped down and joined in.

'Coochy coochy . . .' they all went, tickling Anzac.

'Hehehehehe!" laughed the good-natured dog.

Then Li'l Elvis caught sight of an old man some distance away, between piles of junk. He was bald, with a huge white moustache, and his baggy trousers were kept up with a length of rope instead of a belt.

'Quick, it's Viska!' warned Li'l Elvis.

As Ol' Man Viska approached, the children jumped onto the hollow body of an old car, and Anzac stopped laughing and looked up at them.

'One, two, three — go!' orchestrated Li'l Elvis.

Anzac prepared himself. He cleared his throat and planted his feet wide. Then he threw himself into a frenzy of pure savagery — barking, jumping and snarling. His sharp teeth glinted as though he intended — right now — to attack these children.

'Rargh rargh rarrr rargh rarrr!' he snarled in a most convincing way.

Ol' Man Viska appeared and, once he had seen that the children were safe from Anzac, although huddled together and trembling on the car roof, he smiled proudly.

'Vat a vunderfully vicious doggy!' Ol' Man Viska exclaimed in his eastern European accent. 'You children never learn! You're lucky Anzac didn't sever your extwemities!'

The children performed like professionals. They made their teeth chatter and knees tremble as though they were terrified of Anzac.

'That dog's a menace, Wiska, err Viska,' whimpered Li'l Elvis. 'He scared us half to death.'

Ol' Man Viska smiled and patted his watchdog. 'Good.'

Unseen by Ol' Man Viska, the children winked at Anzac. Taking care not to be seen, the dog grinned back.

The sound of a motor, getting louder, came from the road. A yellow limousine with all sorts of special antennae and aerials pulled to a halt at the front gate of the junkyard.

Now a real change came over Anzac. With a deep frightening growl, he hurled himself towards the limo. He jumped the fence and pushed his fierce muzzle right up against the car's back window, barking viciously.

Safe behind toughened glass, WC Moore, the town's billionaire, stuck out his tongue.

Ol' Man Viska and the children approached, Viska pulling Anzac back. When he was sure that it was safe, and not a moment before, WC pushed a button and his window hummed down. The children hid behind a nearby pile of junk where they were able to hear everything that went on, unseen by WC Moore.

'Viska,' began WC in his usual pompous way, 'tourism is our business in this town and your

savage mutt is jeopardising it all by chasing away innocent tourists!'

'Zat's my boy,' said Ol' Man Viska proudly.

Anzac, too, smiled at the memory of his recent encounters with tourists. He couldn't understand the way they simply stood around and stared. What was the point of that? He trotted away, then found a small log. This gave him an idea. He began to nose it under a back wheel of the limo.

'He's only a dumb animal, Viska,' lectured WC. 'He needs discipline and hard work. That's what got me where I am today!'

The old man looked puzzled. 'Zen lying and cheating had nothing to do with it?'

WC ignored this. 'Viska, all I'm asking is that you chain him up, for his own good.'

Having wedged the log beneath one of the limo's back wheels, Anzac began to push a huge refrigerator from a junk-pile towards the rear of the limo. He wasn't just mean, he was also strong.

WC held up a huge chain and padlock in one hand, and a wad of cash in the other. Ol' Man Viska stared at the chain, then the money.

Money was something he never had enough of.

'You vant me to chain up my doggy?' he asked indignantly. 'I would rather chain up my own mother!'

WC reached into his jacket pocket and added two

more bundles of notes to the one already in his hand. Ol' Man Viska reached out and took the money, smiling. It always paid off to hold out for more.

'All right,' murmured Ol' Man Viska. 'You vant I should chain up my mother as vell?'

WC smiled. Money usually had this effect on people. The limo's engine roared.

'And clean this place up! It looks more like a junkyard every time I see it!' yelled WC.

Duncan, the chauffeur, pushed his foot onto the accelerator. The motor grew loud, but the limo didn't move. So Duncan tried reversing and the car promptly collided with the fridge that Anzac had positioned behind it. The limousine accelerated forward again and went off hissing exhaust fumes from its broken and bent muffler. The children and Anzac had hardly begun to laugh when Viska called out, 'Anzac!'

Everyone was silent. Li'l Elvis and Anzac were looking at one another. Anzac winked at the boy and the children jumped onto the fridge and went back into their terrified routine, as Anzac once again pretended to be a savage watchdog, and jumped and snarled around them.

Ol' Man Viska marched up, clamped the chain on Anzac's red collar, and began to drag him back towards his shack. The children stared at one another, baffled. What was going on? Anzac looked back at them and shrugged with resignation.

'Ol' Man Viska!' called out Li'l Elvis, following with his friends. 'You can't be serious, you're not really chaining him up, are you?'

The old man was shaking his head. 'My vord is my vord, Li'l Elvis. And he does keep on attacking those touvists . . .'

Ol' Man Viska wrapped the chain around a large tree beside his shack and padlocked the links together.

'But you can't just chain him,' protested Lionel. 'Why not train him to be nice to them?'

The old man straightened. 'Anzac has good reason to be vicious, Lionel. Let me tell you a story . . .'

Ol' Man Viska was a good storyteller.

'Ven Anzac was very young,' explained Ol' Man Viska, 'he lived on a farm with all his brothers and sisters . . . Life vas a vattle blossom cooglehoff in those days. Except ven the farmer vas in a bad mood . . .'

A shadow fell across the three puppies. It was the farmer approaching. The mother tried to gather her puppies behind her, to protect them. She managed to get them all except for cheerful Anzac, who, too young to have learnt to be frightened, bounded up to the farmer.

The man looked down. His cheeks and chin were bristly, and a cigarette hung from his bottom lip. Anzac bumped up against his boot and the man picked him up by his tail. After examining him for a moment, as though wondering 'What on earth *is* this thing with four legs and such a happy face?' the farmer threw little Anzac away. The puppy bounced across the hay and whimpered.

Before the farmer left the barn, he dropped his cigarette onto the ground and trod on it carelessly.

The cigarette continued to smoulder and soon the smouldering spread to the straw around it, before turning into flames, which grew rapidly higher, and higher . . .

And as the flames came closer and closer, the terrified puppies huddled around their mother for protection. Anzac looked up and saw a flaming beam start to fall. Too terrified to move, he covered his eyes with his paws. But before the beam could fall onto Anzac, a fireman stepped through a hole where there had once been a wall, and picked up the mother and all the puppies, and carried them to safety.

But Anzac didn't know what had happened — he still had his eyes covered. A shadow fell across him and he opened his eyes. Instead of seeing flames, and approaching death, he saw the farmer. For the

first time in his life, the puppy growled. Sensing the hatred behind the growl, the farmer stepped back.

'And zat's vhy,' Ol' Man Viska concluded his story, 'Anzac hates just about everybody . . . And as for that fireman. Well, that was me. I was that fireman.'

Straining against his new chain, Anzac licked Ol' Man Viska's face. Lionel and Li'l Elvis had tears in their eyes. Moved, though not so tearful, Janet offered them her hanky.

Ol' Man Viska was smiling as he remembered his days with Anzac as a puppy. Then he remembered that he was supposed to be a stern old man.

'Now,' he said gruffly. 'Enough of this sentimental google gar. Get off my property and leave my dog alone!'

Used to Ol' Man Viska and his ways, the children ran off. Anzac, left behind, strained against the chain and looked up at Ol' Man Viska with big, appealing eyes.

'Sorry old fellow,' said Ol' Man Viska, 'but . . . it's for your own good.' And this was true; it wasn't only for the money that Ol' Man Viska had chained up his dog. If Anzac continued to terrify tourists, then sooner or later WC would find a way to get rid of him.

Anzac whimpered. Ol' Man Viska looked away, swallowed, and walked towards his shack. Anzac gazed mournfully down into his water bowl, at his own reflection. A tear fell and broke up the picture.

★ ★ ★

The roadhouse was crowded that afternoon, mainly with tourists bussed in by WC Moore's company, but also with a party of lady bowlers who sat decorously at shiny tables watching L'il Elvis, Janet and Lionel play music that the tourist brochures described as 'the authentic local sound'.

One of few not listening to the music was WC himself, who was at the counter talking to Grace.

'Discipline and hard work,' he was saying, still inspired by his talk with Ol' Man Viska. 'That's what made me what I am today.'

Len passed him a milkshake.

'Yes,' the billionaire continued. 'That's what Li'l Elvis needs. He's running wild, Gracie.'

'A boy his age has to have a little fun,' Grace protested.

WC finished his milkshake in one gigantic slurp and squeezed so hard on it, while sucking, that the metal container buckled. He handed it back to Len for repairs.

'These days,' he went on in his most solemn voice, 'so-called fun is depraved, addictive, computerised, drug-filled, video nasties and ultra-violent, motion picture filth!'

'El isn't like that,' insisted Grace.

The children finished their concert and, amid the applause of the tourists and lady bowlers, jumped from the stage and ran up to Grace.

'Mum,' Li'l Elvis asked in a rush, 'can we go see the "Flames of Hell". It's the new Goondianna Smith movie!'

'Isn't that terribly violent?' Grace wondered, sounding uncertain.

'Just the chainsaw scene . . .' put in Janet.

'Oh yeah!' cried Li'l Elvis. 'Can't wait to see that chainsaw scene!'

He grabbed a knife from the counter and waved it to mimic a slashing chainsaw. But he knocked over a bottle of tomato sauce, which squirted everywhere, just like blood.

This was too much for Grace. 'That's enough!' she said, stamping her foot. 'You're not going to see that film!'

'Why not?' Li'l Elvis wondered.

'Because . . . because you need discipline . . . and hard work!'

'And you need to do two shows a day,' chimed in WC Moore, 'to keep you off the streets!'

'No way!' protested Li'l Elvis.

'Duncan!' yelled WC.

The door to the roadhouse opened and Duncan led in a new party of lady bowlers. The children stared, aghast.

'What a coincidence,' said WC. 'Another tourist bus, just waiting there! We're in luck.'

Just like Anzac, Li'l Elvis growled, 'Grrrrrr . . .'

WC took this hint, and began to treat the boy just as if he were a dog. Li'l Elvis still had his electric guitar over his shoulder. WC grabbed the power cord and pulled him back to the stage. Li'l Elvis howled like a dog. His friends followed reluctantly. The lady bowlers stared expectantly at the stage.

That night, Li'l Elvis had one of his worst nightmares ever. He saw himself playing his guitar on the roadhouse stage, except that his guitar was making a whining noise, like a chained-up dog. Then, with an evil laugh, WC came along and clamped a spiked dog-collar just like Anzac's around his neck.

'No! No!' Li'l Elvis had cried out in his sleep.

And however hard he struggled, and no matter what he did, he had been unable to get the dog-collar off.

He had woken with his sheet wound around his neck, like a real collar. But his relief that the whole thing had only been a dream quickly faded, though, when he heard Anzac's lonely howling.

He disentangled himself from the sheet and went to the window. He could just make out the dog, between distant piles of junk, howling at the moon. From his nightmare, Li'l Elvis knew what it was like to be chained up. In sympathy for poor Anzac, he felt as if he were going to cry.

He suddenly knew that it was up to him to do something about all this.

At night the junkyard became a place of shadowy shapes all doing their best to imitate something dangerous. Li'l Elvis, Janet and Lionel crept from junk pile to junk pile, creeping towards Anzac.

'Quiff Boy,' whispered Lionel, 'this may be your dumbest idea ever — and it's got plenty of competition.'

Li'l Elvis halted and his voice was urgent with feeling. 'We can't just let WC turn Anzac's life into misery. If we train Anzac to be nice to everyone, then he'll be free.'

Lionel sighed and shook his head. Around the next pile of junk they saw Anzac sitting still and looking totally miserable. When he saw the children he started to give a joyful yelp, but Li'l Elvis, who had come prepared for this, threw a huge bone into the dog's mouth to muffle the sound. He put his finger to his lips.

'Shhhhh.'

Anzac understood and nodded. Lionel followed the chain until he came to a huge padlock.

He turned to Anzac. 'Where does Ol' Man Viska keep the key?'

Anzac pointed straight to Ol' Man Viska's shack. The children crept over, and saw Ol' Man Viska lying fast asleep on a bed beneath the window, snoring heavily. He had on a white nightcap and with each snore his moustache fluttered at its ends. The key was hanging from a nail on the shelf just above his head.

Li'l Elvis leant in and reached for the key.

He found himself leaning so far forward, with the key still just out of reach, that if he didn't grab onto something he would fall on Ol' Man Viska's face. He reached for a shelf crowded with vases and pots, and just caught the edge of it. But it tilted, and the things on it slid to the edge, threatening to tumble onto the old man's head.

The boys gasped. But this was no time for thinking of all the dreadful things that might happen.

Taking a great risk, Li'l Elvis pushed just a fraction harder on the shelf and at the same time grabbed the key off the hook. The boys scrambled outside.

When Janet saw them and the key, she was about to say 'Hooray' when Lionel clapped his hand over her mouth. 'Hoorammph,' she said instead.

'Piece of cake,' whispered Li'l Elvis.

They closed the window as gently as they could, but this was just enough, with Li'l Elvis's push of a moment ago, to send the shelf tipping down towards Ol' Man Viska, making the vases and pots cascade onto his head.

The old man sat upright and clunked his head on the shelf, both pushing the shelf back to its correct position and knocking himself back into sleepiness.

'Errr ... Gotta do zose renovations ...' he muttered, as he drifted back into unconsciousness.

Li'l Elvis fitted the key into the padlock and turned it. When he stood up, Janet was threading a length of rope through Anzac's collar.

'What's that for?' Li'l Elvis wondered. Had they freed him from a chain in order to tie him up with a rope?

Janet shrugged. 'Just a precaution. He's been chained up all day and night, so there's a chance he might go ...'

Li'l Elvis took the chain off Anzac's collar and the dog immediately shot off at near the speed of light, dragging Janet behind him.

'BERSERK!' cried Janet, finishing her sentence.

Anzac and Janet flew over the fence. Li'l Elvis and Lionel looked down at the rapidly diminishing coil of rope.

'Do you think we should . . . ?' Li'l Elvis wondered.

'Give her a hand?' Lionel finished.

Completely underestimating the strength and speed of the dog, they reached down, grabbed the rope, and were immediately yanked into the distance.

On the way into the town, Janet spotted an abandoned sheet of corrugated iron. As quickly as she could, she planted her feet on it, and from now on she had a makeshift sled. The boys caught up by pulling themselves along the rope and joined her on the sled. Now it was almost fun, whizzing through the town, pulled by a dog busy getting over the horror of being chained up. They slid down Main Street and went twice around the roundabout and the golden statue of WC.

This new form of transportation, combined with the dark and silent night, made Li'l Elvis wonder. For an instant he closed his eyes and imagined the town covered in snow, and a Santa Claus-like figure whipping down Main Street in a sled pulled by reindeer. On the back was a whole pile of stuff, a guitar case right at the top. Outside the roadhouse the sled swerved and the guitar case fell off, onto the doorstep with the lid bumping open, and there was Li'l Elvis inside, as a baby, clothed in animal skins.

'I wonder,' Li'l Elvis murmured, 'if that's the way it happened on the night I was found . . .'

He opened his eyes when he heard Lionel and Janet scream. They were heading for the abandoned army barracks. Anzac changed direction just in time, and ran around and around a large tree. The rope caught the trunk and, as the children held onto each other and began to whimper, Anzac and the sled whipped around in different directions . . . until finally everyone collided with the tree.

When they had picked themselves up, Li'l Elvis looked down at the dog and decided to leave him just where he was — roped to the tree.

'This is for your own good, Anzac,' he explained. 'I know what it's like to be chained up all the time. Tomorrow we begin Operation Nice Doggy!'

Anzac barked, eager for anything that involved being with Li'l Elvis Jones and the Truckstoppers.

But Lionel and Janet groaned, knowing only too well how Li'l Elvis's plans generally turned out.

'I can hardly wait . . .' said Janet.

Lionel and Janet went to Li'l Elvis's place the next morning. After their adventures of last night all three children found it difficult to keep their eyes open and their heads from falling onto the table.

With the skill born of many years' practice, Len was flipping eggs and sausages directly from a frying pan to the plates on the table. As each item of food landed, Lionel stirred himself, brought up his didgeridoo, and sucked it up. Li'l Elvis and Janet, though, with nothing to do, had just about fallen fast asleep when Grace appeared with a plate of toast.

'Hmmm,' she said. 'If I didn't know better, I'd say you three had been up all night.'

'What . . . ?' asked Li'l Elvis, stirring himself. 'No, Mum, we're fine. We're just hungry.'

Len shrugged when he saw the empty plates behind him, then turned resignedly to cook some more.

'Nothing worse than running on empty,' he commented. 'There you go, start your engines.'

He flipped more sausages onto the plates, which Lionel promptly sucked up. When Len and Grace glanced at the table a second later, and saw that the food had already gone, they staggered back with surprise, and looked questioningly at their son.

'Any chance of seconds?' asked Li'l Elvis.

★　★　★

The children rushed to the abandoned army barracks. Anzac, freed from his rope, jumped happily around them. And he could smell something too . . . something tasty . . .

They went inside one of the huts and Lionel raised the didge to his mouth, blew into it, and out came bacon, eggs and sausages, all in a huge pile.

'Well Anzac, go for —' But before Janet could finish her sentence, Anzac had swallowed the whole lot in a few lightning-fast gulps. He gave a loud burp of satisfaction and wagged his tail. 'Okay, so what's the next treat?' he seemed to be saying.

'You sure you not part pig?' Lionel asked the dog.

'Okay!' Li'l Elvis wanted to get things started. 'Time for Anzac's first training session.'

Anzac was excited by all this attention. Usually he was by himself in the junkyard. He proceeded to sit up, beg, shake the children's hands, and to roll over and play dead. He sat up expectantly, to see if he had the children's approval. But Li'l Elvis only shook his head.

'No, we're not here to teach you tricks. We're going to teach you how to be . . . nice.'

Lionel brought an easel from the far corner of the room, covered by a cloth.

'Now, Anzac,' he said, 'if we can train you to like the nastiest person in town, you'll theoretically like anybody.'

Anzac nodded as if he knew exactly what was going on.

Lionel pulled the cover from the easel. On a large piece of paper they had drawn the picture of a fat man carrying a milkshake container and wearing a yellow suit and purple shirt. It was WC Moore. Anzac began to growl savagely.

'Grrrrrr.'

'Calm down, boy!' Li'l Elvis begged. 'I know it's ugly, but it's just a diagram, okay?'

Anzac managed to calm himself down, a bit.

Lionel began his lecture. 'Now, being "nice" to WC Moore has many advantages. For example, he may offer you a sip from his milkshake . . .' Lionel pointed to the milkshake on the diagram, '. . . or give you a biscuit from his pocket.' He pointed to WC's pockets. 'So don't think rump steak, Anzac, think "WC is my friend, WC is my friend".'

But Anzac was already thinking the wrong thing. As he stared at WC he began to think of sausages, and steak, and . . .

He leapt at the diagram and tore it to pieces.

There was a silence.

'Maybe we should move onto the next phase,' suggested Lionel.

They slid the easel away. In another corner Lionel had connected his laptop computer to wires, a washing line and a pulley. He pressed the 'enter' key and out from behind a sheet came a WC Moore dummy, life-size, made from old sacks and clothes filched from their homes. The dummy travelled towards Anzac, pulled by overhead wires.

Anzac snarled.

Lionel spoke into the microphone on his computer, so that the words appeared to be coming from the dummy.

'Hello! I just want to be your friend.'

Again, despite his huge breakfast, Anzac couldn't think of WC as anything but a collection of cuts of meat. He didn't merely want to bite WC, he wanted to gobble him completely up.

He dived for the throat of the dummy and set about the business of ripping it to pieces. Stuffing, wires and ripped clothes flew everywhere. Lionel, Janet and Li'l Elvis stood back and looked at one another. There was no point trying to stop Anzac when he was like this.

'Maybe if it had a different voice?' suggested Lionel hopefully.

So they patched up the dummy and Li'l Elvis went to the microphone.

'Hello again!' he called out, pretending to be WC. 'I know we got off to a bad start but . . .'

Anzac again flew at the dummy, this time completely destroying it.

'Time for Plan B . . .' said Lionel.

They placed Anzac on a chair, and while Li'l Elvis held onto his collar and Janet held the dog's jaws shut, Lionel stood in front of him, holding a huge spiral lollipop. He waved it from side to side and spoke as slowly and carefully as he could.

'You are getting sleepy . . . sleeeeeeeepy. You will listen and obey.'

Anzac stared obediently at the lollipop. At least it didn't look like WC.

'You will not bite tourists anymore,' intoned Lionel. 'You are a nice, friendly little doggy.'

'I will not bite tourists anymore. I am a nice, friendly little doggy,' said Li'l Elvis, who was staring straight ahead, wide eyed, in a hypnotic trance.

Now that Lionel had stopped swinging the lollipop around, Anzac seized the opportunity to bite it off its stick and swallow it in one gulp. He jumped down from his chair and barked excitedly at Li'l Elvis.

'Ruff, ruff, ruff!'

Like a good little doggy, Li'l Elvis barked back. 'Ruff, ruff, ruff!'

The boy and dog frisked around, each happy to have found a new friend.

Unnoticed by the children, unnoticed even by Anzac, someone was watching all this. It was Spike, giving a mischievous grin as he peered in through the window of the hut.

Janet and Lionel took Li'l Elvis outside and, to end his trance, threw a bucketful of water onto his head. Li'l Elvis seemed not at all startled by this. He merely shook himself, like a dog and stood up.

'Okay, El,' Janet asked. 'Who are you?'

Li'l Elvis frowned with concentration. 'I am a nice, happy little ... little ...' And then he remembered: 'Little Elvis.'

Janet and Lionel sighed with relief.

'And boy, I could go a dog biscuit,' he joked.

'Ha! Ha!' came a scrapey voice from the window ledge above their heads. 'Smelvis is a dog! Smelvis is a dog!'

Spike jumped down.

'What do you want, Lizard Breath?' Li'l Elvis asked.

'I saw you!' Spike accused. 'Trying to make Anzac into a wimp! When Ol' Man Viska finds out he's gonna be *really mad*!'

It didn't take long for the three children to corner Spike against the hut. They pushed up against him, threateningly.

'Nice T-shirt you got there, Spike,' said Li'l Elvis.

Spike puffed out his chest, not catching Li'l Elvis's tone at all. The picture on his T-shirt showed the action hero, Goondi Smith, surrounded by leaping flames.

'Yeah!' agreed Spike. 'Goondi Smith and the Flames From Hell!'

'Very nice,' said Li'l Elvis, trying to make his voice as menacing as possible. 'Be a real shame if Anzac bit a big hole in it.'

Spike suddenly understood what was going on. He was being threatened.

He swallowed.

★   ★   ★

Back at the roadhouse, Grace was getting worried. Lady bowlers were filing in, but where were Li'l Elvis and his band? As her husband made milkshakes, Grace looked at her watch.

'Len,' she asked, 'do you think two shows a day is too hard on the kids?'

'Too late now, Gracie, call them in.'

So Gracie went to the front door and raised her hands to her mouth.

'LI'L EL-VIS! SHOW TIME!' she shrieked, making a huge noise for such a small woman.

Li'l Elvis and his friends winced as they heard Grace's shout. Spike grinned.

'If doing one show wasn't bad enough,' Li'l Elvis lamented, 'now it's two. Just remember, Spike — being mauled by a junkyard dog can ruin your entire day.'

With that, the children jumped on their scootboards and sped off, leaving Spike to regain his self-confidence.

'Yeah?' he demanded of no one in particular. 'Well, if you can train Anzac to *like* people, I can just train him to *unlike* them!'

Li'l Elvis and the Truckstoppers climbed wearily onto the roadhouse's little stage. As tourists, lady bowlers, WC and others looked on, they launched into a tired-sounding performance without even tuning their instruments.

And by the time they had reached the second number they were even more tired. One of Janet's drumsticks bounced away, but she kept on drumming anyway, not even noticing the difference.

Lionel's eyes were closed and he seemed to be playing his didgeridoo while fast asleep. Li'l Elvis leant to one side, then to the other, but when you are tired, and standing up, it's difficult to get comfortable.

Observing all this through the eyes of a worried mother, Grace frowned at WC. But the rich man was busily counting bags of money.

'I'm really not sure,' said Grace, 'about these two shows a day. They look so tired . . . '

'You know what's making them tired?' replied WC, glancing away from his money for the briefest possible time. 'Computer games and video nasties!'

On stage, the children had finished their set of songs. They bowed as the audience applauded.

And then they simply stayed there, with their heads bowed, while everyone else started to look increasingly mystified.

Janet dropped her remaining drumstick onto her foot and this was enough to wake her. Startled, she woke the others, and they all raced off to the door to resume their training of Anzac.

But WC was waiting for them, blocking the exit with his huge bulk.

'Where are you kids going?' he demanded. 'Show number two is about to begin. Duncan!'

WC's wretched chauffeur opened the roadhouse door, and as the bowling ladies shuffled out, a whole busload of tourists poured in.

WC led the children back to the stage, saying, 'Discipline and hard work! It's for your own good!'

While the children wearily played and sang for the tourists, Ol' Man Viska was wandering sadly down main street.

'Anzac, Anzac, all is forgiven!' he called out.

He looked in rubbish bins and down alleys and lanes. Finally he got down on his knees and started sniffing for Anzac's scent. No, Anzac hadn't been around here.

He stood up and bowed his head.

'Oh Anzac. I miss you so . . .'

Anzac was at the army barracks, fast asleep. Above him, Spike was hanging from the electric light cord in the ceiling, holding a fishing rod with a bone tied to the line. He grinned in anticipation of the fun he was about to have.

'Wakey, wakey,' he called out. 'Anzac! You dumb dog . . .'

Spike lowered the bone close to Anzac's nose.

The dog woke up, sniffing. Before he was even properly awake, he snapped at the bone. But at the last second it zipped away and Anzac bit empty space. He looked up and shook his head. He must have misjudged the distance. Strange, he didn't normally do that. He pounced and chomped again. The bone darted away. Watching the high-speed bone carefully, Anzac crouched, ready to spring.

This time the bone started moving before Anzac even moved. He chased it, tearing around the room. He nearly caught it when it suddenly jerked upwards. He jumped and caught it, only to find himself hanging in mid-air.

For the first time, Anzac noticed the fishing line attached to the bone. He followed this with his eyes, up, up . . . to the fishing rod.

He followed this to Spike's hands, arms and last of all to Spike's malicious grin.

'Grrrr,' went Anzac, when he understood what had been happening.

'Ooops,' said Spike, dropping the rod so that both the bone and Anzac fell to the floor. Then Spike lost his grip on the electric cord and began to fall too. This was something he hadn't planned. But he caught sight of a ladder over against a wall and, before Anzac could untangle himself from the fishing line, he raced up it.

His malicious grin returned. 'Haw haw! What's a matter dog? Too dumb to climb a ladder?'

But Anzac was far cleverer than Spike could have guessed. He looked coolly at both Spike and the ladder, then sauntered over and took a bite out of one of the ladder's legs. Then he stepped back, and a few paces to one side, and waited.

Spike laughed. 'What are you gonna do, eat the whole ladder? What a dumb dog.'

Unbalanced, the ladder started to keel over.

'Whoooah!' Spike cried.

Anzac had positioned himself exactly where the ladder was about to land. He grinned and opened his mouth.

'Yeeeeargh!' cried Spike, seeing the dog's teeth get closer and closer. He put his hands over his face, now resigned to being eaten alive by the dog he had taken such pleasure in tormenting.

Just as Spike was about to land, Anzac saw the flames on the boy's T-shirt, and the sight of these took him back to that time in the barn, with the flaming beam falling. He couldn't control himself — the fear inspired by that memory overcame him. He backed away from the T-shirt and covered his head with his paws.

Spike landed right in front of the Anzac, but the dog only whimpered. He opened one eye a fraction,

but saw nothing but the flames of the T-shirt and closed it again immediately.

Once he was sure that he wasn't about to be bitten, Spike grinned.

'Ha! Smelvis turned you into a real wuss. C'mon, fight like a dog.'

Certain that the dog was a coward and that he wasn't taking any risk at all, Spike got down on all fours and made as if to bite the dog. Anzac cowered away, paws still over his eyes.

Eventually, Spike tired of this game.

'Ahh, ya bore me!' he said, slamming the door of the hut behind him.

Anzac retreated to a corner and whimpered, waiting for the fears of his puppyhood to go away.

The second performance of the day by Li'l Elvis and the Truckstoppers was going even worse than the first. As the tourists and lady bowlers watched, Janet began to drum slower and slower, until finally she fell asleep with a loud crash onto her cymbals.

This completely failed to stir the others. Lionel leant on his didgeridoo and fell fast asleep. Li'l Elvis strummed his guitar aimlessly for a few more seconds, before slumping over his microphone and snoring. The microphone made it sound like a thousand pigs grunting at the top of their voices.

The tourists stared. What sort of 'authentic local music' was this?

WC ran onto the stage. 'Ahem,' he called out. 'We seem to be having some technical difficulties, which I assure you will be rectified by the third show, later today.'

This was quite enough for Grace. Third show? No one had told her anything about that.

She marched up to the stage. 'There will be no third show and from now on there will be no second show!' she announced.

'But, but,' protested WC, 'it's for their own good.'

Beside him, Li'l Elvis had begun to slide to the floor.

'Look!' WC pointed out. 'They're keen.'

He rushed around and tried to put the drumsticks back into Janet's hands. But her head remained on the cymbals and her hands refused to move. Then WC wrapped his hands around the didgeridoo and tried to move the boy's head up to the top. But Lionel drooped down immediately.

'No!' cried Grace indignantly. 'This isn't about Li'l Elvis's good, it's about your bank balance! I'd rather Li'l Elvis stayed the boy he is, instead of the cash register you want him to be!'

Li'l Elvis stirred. His mother's strident voice had woken him up.

'You'd rather . . . I stayed the boy I am?' As he realised what this meant, he sat up straighter. 'Yeah!'

His mother hugged him, but before either could say anything else, Ol' Man Viska wandered into the roadhouse.

'Anzac?' he called out forlornly. 'Has anybody seen my Anzac?'

Li'l Elvis suddenly realised what he had to do. He ran straight up to the old man.

'And Anzac's gotta be who he is, too! I've made a big mistake,' he explained.

Ol' Man Viska, who had no idea what the boy was talking about, only stared.

Together, Li'l Elvis, Janet, Lionel and Ol' Man Viska rushed from the roadhouse to the barracks. As Li'l Elvis opened the door to the hut, they all heard a whimpering, then a long low whine.

As they entered, Anzac cowered further away.

'Anzac!' said Ol' Man Viska softly. 'Vhere's all your viciousness gone?'

'He was his usual vicious self when we left him, honest,' Li'l Elvis assured the old man.

As the children, Viska and Anzac walked back down Main Street, Dotty and Lotty were sweeping the footpath outside their general store. They looked up, nodded to Ol' Man Viska, to the children, and then saw Anzac.

That dog! Possibly the most savage dog the world had ever known! They froze, too frightened to think properly, then ran into their shop and locked the door after them.

The next to panic were Hector and Victor, out the front of their shop playing cards. Victor saw Anzac first, and muttered under his breath, 'The dog'.

Both were gone in an instant, into the Paragon Café, leaving cards, table and chairs behind them.

Anzac certainly did have a reputation in Little Memphis.

Further down the street was WC's limousine. The instant Duncan caught sight of the dog, he crawled underneath it as fast as he could.

Spike was playing marbles with WC. They both looked up at the same time and saw . . . Anzac.

'Oh no . . .' whispered the billionaire.

Spike grinned. Here was his chance to prove himself a hero before the whole town.

'Relax, watch this,' he said as he swaggered, showing no sign of fear, towards Anzac.

As Spike approached, the dog hardly had time to

start a snarl before he caught sight of the printed flames on the T-shirt. He darted behind Ol' Man Viska's legs and cringed.

Spike laughed. 'Ha ha! Are you a mongrel or a mouse? Squeak up!'

Everyone — very slowly, very cautiously — was starting to come out of their shops.

WC smiled. At last, the tourist-biter tamed!

'So the mutt's lost his bite, eh?' he said to Ol' Man Viska. 'In that case, I'll have my money back!'

Viska scowled and said nothing.

WC's smile grew even smugger. 'Excuse us, won't you, we have a marble game to finish.'

With a casual gesture, he sent his high-powered Berkonium marble zinging through the air to knock all the marbles out of the circle and straight into his pocket. The loyal marble itself shot straight back to its home on WC's ring.

'Two out of three?' he asked Spike.

'You're on.'

They began to set up their marbles again.

This was too much for Li'l Elvis to bear. 'I've got to do something,' he muttered, dropping to his knees beside Anzac. 'Come on,' he exhorted. 'Stand up to them! You can do it!'

'It's no good.' Ol' Man Viska was shaking his head sadly. 'You have killed his spirit.'

Spike laughed and Li'l Elvis looked up, trying to think of a really wonderful insult to hurl at him.

Then he saw the 'Flames from Hell' T-shirt and remembered the story that Ol' Man Viska had told of Anzac's puppyhood.

'The flames!' he said to himself, getting to his feet and sprinting over to Spike.

Before the other boy could do anything to defend himself, Li'l Elvis had torn off the flame-patterned shirt.

'Argh!' screamed Spike, mystified at why anyone would want to rip off his T-shirt.

But Li'l Elvis had already returned to Anzac. 'See, Anzac,' he appealed. 'See, it's not real fire.'

He brought the T-shirt right up to the dog's nose, then waved it around.

Anzac frowned with concentration, then, far down in his throat, a highly dangerous growl began.

'Grrrrr . . .'

Anzac lunged at the T-shirt and took about half a second to tear it into shreds.

Spike's sneering expression had completely gone. As Anzac regained his old savagery, the boy's eyes widened, and his knees began to shake. If he stayed still another moment, he would be too terrified even to run. So he swung around, and ran faster than he had ever done in his life.

Anzac followed, growling ultra-fiercely.

Spike clambered up a lamppost, but Anzac was there in time to bite off one of his boots. Spike continued to climb and Anzac gave a growl of frustration. He had been so looking forward to gobbling someone up.

All the people who had started to come out of their shops had firmly gone in again, and locked their doors. Anzac looked all around and had nearly begun to despair when he saw something very much to his taste. In fact, it was more than he could have hoped for. It was a dream come true.

WC was bending right over, facing away from Anzac. He was absorbed in the marbles, moving from side to side in search of the perfect angle.

Anzac stared at the billionaire's bulging buttocks and sprang.

'AAAAArrrrrggggghhhhh!!!!' cried WC, as teeth fastened around the seat of his pants.

Ol' Man Viska and Li'l Elvis gave each other a smile.

'Zat's my boy,' said the old man approvingly, nodding at Anzac's savage behaviour.

With the dog snapping at his legs, WC raced for, and began to climb, the lamppost.

'Viska!' he shrieked, once he was at the top huddled next to Spike. 'I'll sue you for this!'

Anzac barked a cheerful hello to his master and settled down to chomp his way through the lamppost.

'I don't care!' the junkyard proprietor answered the billionaire happily. 'I've got my Anzac back!'

Also available from HarperCollins*Publishers*

Book One
ISBN: 0 207 19659 1

Book Two
ISBN: 0 207 19658 3

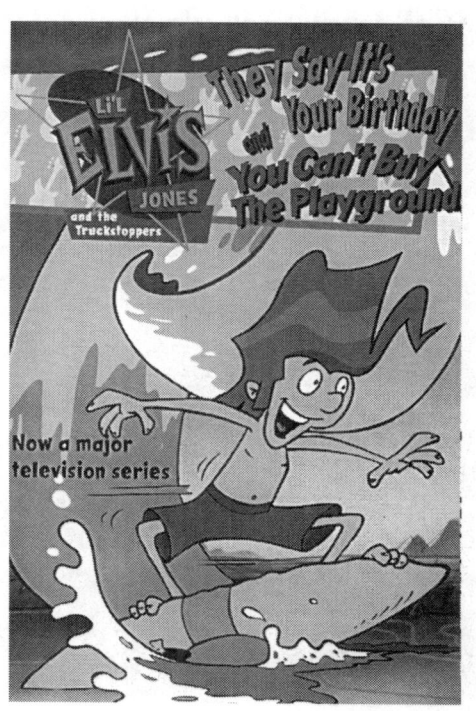

Book Three
ISBN: 0 207 19657 5

Now you can watch your favourite television series on video.
Four volumes in the first series.